TRAVELING
TO
TONDO

A Tale of the Nkundo of Zaire

Retold by VERNA AARDEMA

Illustrated by WILL HILLENBRAND

ALFRED A. KNOPF

NEW YORK

To my great-grandson Nicolas Adsit,

who arrived before this book

V. A.

For Joshua

W. H.

Traveling to Tondo: A Tale of the Nkundo of Zaire is a retelling by Verna Aardema of Tale 95, with one episode from Tale 14,
in *"On Another Day...": Tales Told Among the Nkundo of Zaire,* by Mabel H. Ross and Barbara K. Walker,
published by The Shoe String Press, Inc., Hamden, Connecticut, 1979.

THIS IS A BORZOI BOOK PUBLISHED BY ALFRED A. KNOPF, INC.

Text copyright © 1991 by Verna Aardema. Illustrations copyright © 1991 by Will Hillenbrand
All rights reserved under International and Pan-American Copyright Conventions. Published in the United States
by Alfred A. Knopf, Inc., New York, and simultaneously in Canada by Random House of Canada Limited, Toronto.
Distributed by Random House, Inc., New York.
Book design by Elizabeth Hardie. Manufactured in Singapore 2 4 6 8 0 9 7 5 3 1

Library of Congress Cataloging-in-Publication Data
Aardema, Verna. Traveling to Tondo / by Verna Aardema : illustrated by Will Hillenbrand.
p. cm.
Summary: On his way to his wedding, with his friends as attendants, a civet cat meets with extraordinary and unexpected delays.
ISBN 0-679-80081-6 (trade) 0-679-90081-0 (lib. bdg.)   [1. Folklore–Zaire.] I. Hillenbrand, Will, ill. II. Title. PZ8.1.A213Tr 1991
398.2'452974422'096751—dc20   90-39419 CIP AC

GLOSSARY and GUIDE TO PRONUNCIATION

(in order of occurrence)

Tondo (TON-doh): A town on Lake Tumba

Nkundo (uhn-KOON-doh): People who live in the rain forest of Zaire; their language
    is called Lonkundo (Lon-KOON-doh)

Bowane (boh-WAH-nay): Lonkundo for civet cat

Embenga (em-BENG-ga): Lonkundo for pigeon

ika-o (ee-KAH-oh)

bwa-wa (BWAH-wah)

Nguma (uhn-GOO-mah): Lonkundo for python

swe-o (SWAY-oh)

Ulu (OO-loo): Lonkundo for tortoise

ta-ka (TAH-kah)

a-o (AH-oh)

ngo-nga (uhn-GOH-uhn-GAH)

pa-o (PAH-oh)

N-YEH (nyeh): Lonkundo for no or never, and traditionally spelled nye

Muh! (muh!): An expression of disgust, traditionally spelled mu!

One day in the town of Tondo, Bowane the civet cat met a beautiful feline he wanted for a wife. The cat was willing. And her father agreed to the marriage and set a certain bride price.

Bowane returned to his own animal village.
Soon he acquired the copper bars and
ornaments he needed. And early one morning,
with the bridewealth in a basket, he set out to
fetch his bride.

Then there was

Bowane walking, *ika-o, ika-o, ika-o*—
All alone, traveling to Tondo.

Bowane needed attendants to go with him. So he went to the home of his friend Embenga the pigeon and called, "Embenga, are you awake?"

Embenga peeked out of his small doorway. "Yes. I am awake."

Bowane said, "Come go with me to Tondo. There I shall marry a beautiful cat, and I need you to attend me."

"Between friends there is only goodness," said Embenga. "I will go with you."

Then there were

Bowane walking, *ika-o, ika-o, ika-o;*

And Embenga flapping, *bwa-wa, bwa-wa, bwa-wa*—

The two of them traveling to Tondo.

Next they went to the home of Nguma the python. Bowane called, "Nguma, are you there?"

Nguma poked his head out of his doorway. "Yes. I am here."

Bowane said, "Come go with us to Tondo. There I shall marry a beautiful cat. And I need you to attend me."

Nguma grumbled, "To Tondo! That's a day's journey! Why didn't you fall in love close by? But since you are my friend, I will go with you."

Then there were

    Bowane walking, *ika-o, ika-o, ika-o;*

    Embenga flapping, *bwa-wa, bwa-wa, bwa-wa;*

    And Nguma slithering, *swe-o, swe-o, swe-o—*

The three of them traveling to Tondo.

Last they went to the home of Ulu the tortoise. Ulu was in his yard mending a fishing net.

Bowane said, "Ulu, come go with us to Tondo. There I shall marry a beautiful cat. And I need you to attend me."

"Oh, a wedding!" said Ulu. "I never miss a wedding. Of course, I will join you."

Then there were

Bowane walking, *ika-o, ika-o, ika-o;*

Embenga flapping, *bwa-wa, bwa-wa, bwa-wa;*

Nguma slithering, *swe-o, swe-o, swe-o;*

And Ulu waddling, *ta-ka, ta-ka, ta-ka, ta-ka—*

The four of them traveling to Tondo.

Presently the travelers came to a waterhole. The pigeon, the python, and the tortoise began to drink, *a-o, a-o, a-o.*

The civet cat was thirsty too. But he said, "It is taboo for me to drink water except from my own dish. Wait here. I will return home and fetch it."

His friends said, "No matter. That is all right."

So while they waited at the waterhole, Bowane went back home. After a long time he returned. "See, I have come already," he said. And he filled his dish and drank.

Then they went on—

    Bowane walking, *ika-o, ika-o, ika-o;*
    Embenga flapping, *bwa-wa, bwa-wa, bwa-wa;*
    Nguma slithering, *swe-o, swe-o, swe-o;*
    And Ulu waddling, *ta-ka, ta-ka, ta-ka, ta-ka—*
The four of them traveling to Tondo.

At length, they came to a palm tree that was loaded with nuts. Embenga was all aflutter, *bwa-wa, bwa-wa.* But the palm nuts were not ripe.

Embenga said, "Stay here, my friends, until the nuts are ready to eat. You know we pigeons like nothing better than ripe palm nuts."

"No matter," said Bowane. And the others said, "It is all right."

So they stayed near the palm tree for two whole weeks while the nuts ripened, and Embenga ate them.

Then they went on—
Bowane walking, *ika-o, ika-o, ika-o;*
Embenga flapping, *bwa-wa, bwa-wa, bwa-wa;*
Nguma slithering, *swe-o, swe-o, swe-o;*
And Ulu waddling, *ta-ka, ta-ka, ta-ka, ta-ka—*
The four of them traveling to Tondo.

Farther on, Nguma caught a small antelope. He squeezed it
and licked it. Then, A-OOOOOH! He swallowed it all in one piece.

And he said, "My friends, when I swallow an animal, I cannot travel until the digestion is finished. We must rest here."

"No matter," said Bowane. And the others said, "It is all right."

Day after day, the travelers waited and watched, watched and waited, as the lump in the python grew smaller. Finally it was gone. And Nguma said, "Arise. I can travel now."

And so they went on—

Bowane walking, *ika-o, ika-o, ika-o;*

Embenga flapping, *bwa-wa, bwa-wa, bwa-wa;*

Nguma slithering, *swe-o, swe-o, swe-o;*

And Ulu waddling, *ta-ka, ta-ka, ta-ka, ta-ka*—

The four of them traveling to Tondo.

At last they reached a forest that was near their destination. But there, blocking the path, was a huge fallen tree. The civet cat and the python climbed over it. The pigeon flew over it.

But the tortoise scrabbled up a little way and then fell back, *ngo-nga*. He did that again and again. Finally he gave up and said, "My friends, I am not able to climb over this big tree trunk. We must stay here until it rots, so that I can cross."

Bowane cried, "We cannot do that! When would we ever get to Tondo?"

Nguma echoed, "We cannot do that!"

And Embenga shook his small head and said, "N-YEH, N-YEH!"

But Ulu protested, "I waited for all of you! Why do you complain when you have to wait for me?"

So they stayed there in the forest year after year, while the tree trunk rotted away. And one day Ulu said, "At last! It is time to rejoice. The log has crumbled."

And *pa-o, pa-o, pa-o,* he climbed over the mound.

Then the friends continued their journey. And soon they emerged from the forest and entered the town of Tondo.

Straight to the home of the bride they went.

He called, "I, Bowane, have come!"

The beautiful cat Bowane had come to marry appeared at the door. "Muh!" she cried. "How dare you show your face after all these years? Did you think I would wait forever?"

Just then two civet kittens came tumbling out of the doorway beside her. "I married someone else," she said. "And these are my children."

"Oh," said Bowane sadly. Then he explained, "My friends waited for me to get my water dish. We waited for Embenga's nuts to ripen. We waited for Nguma's food to digest. And we waited for a log to rot so that Ulu could pass."

"You waited for a log to rot!" she cried.
"How could you be so foolish! Now you and
your friends be gone, or I'll call my husband."
Then out from behind her came the biggest
civet cat Bowane and his friends had ever seen.
And he was baring his teeth, *NNNNNNN!*

Suddenly there were
    Bowane running, *ikaoikaoikao;*
    Embenga flying, *bwawabwawabwawa;*
    Nguma streaking, *sweosweosweo;*
    And Ulu scurrying, *takatakatakataka*—
The four of them hurrying home from Tondo.
    As in this story, sometimes between
friends there is too much consenting. If a thing
is not wise to do, it is best to say, "N-YEH!"

Aardema, Verna.
Traveling to Tondo.

$12.95